POEMS

Mystery of her Magic

VENKYY

BLUEROSE PUBLISHERS
India | U.K.

Copyright © Venkatesh Ambati 2024

All rights reserved by author. No part of this publication may be reproduced, stored in a retrieval system or transmitted in any form or by any means, electronic, mechanical, photocopying, recording or otherwise, without the prior permission of the author. Although every precaution has been taken to verify the accuracy of the information contained herein, the publisher assumes no responsibility for any errors or omissions. No liability is assumed for damages that may result from the use of information contained within.

BlueRose Publishers takes no responsibility for any damages, losses, or liabilities that may arise from the use or misuse of the information, products, or services provided in this publication.

For permissions requests or inquiries regarding this publication, please contact:

BLUEROSE PUBLISHERS
www.BlueRoseONE.com
info@bluerosepublishers.com
+91 8882 898 898
+4407342408967

ISBN: 978-93-6452-033-1

Cover design: Shivam
Typesetting: Namrata Saini

First Edition: July 2024

For Julie,

you're the closest to heaven that I'll ever be.

I have been astonished that men could die martyrs for their religion--

I have shuddered at it,

I shudder no more.

I could be martyred for my religion.

Love is my religion and I could die for that.

I could die for you.

- John Keats

Contents

Sight of Mystery 1

Sight of Love 45

Sight of Magic 103

Sight of Mystery

She sway her hairs
and I am caught up
in her perfume like a bee
who has found its perfect flower.

The love of yours was like a shining star
in the bubble of his obscure life.

She was the best friend I ever had the
one that took care of me on the nights
I abhorred myself

*And one day
I saw her smile
and I knew
at last my heart
has found its home.*

She came to me like
the first few raindrops
before the storm — little by little
then all at once.

She curbed every scar
on his heart
every piece he hated
about himself
and with that
she healed him
with her magic.

She sat quietly in a room full of art
doing nothing and everything
at the same time
in a way that if anyone enters
they would start dreaming of
becoming a poet just by looking at her.

Mystery of her Magic

The thing about her is that
she has this extraordinary ability
to make you believe that magic exists
just by her presence.

It was the moment when you paused
and we sat there in silence of it all,
I knew, we are in love —
because love resides
in the pauses of our talks.

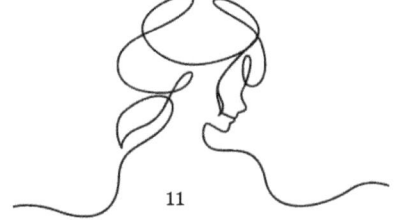

I was drunk on her **AURA** which has the power to heal this broken world.

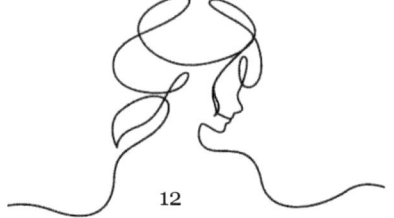

The day I saw her in white
where every bird was
singing with delight
in awe of her smile
the winds were fighting
to flow around her sight,
for them
they know that this magic of her
will be once and for all
and for those who are lucky enough
to feel her like I do.

And sometimes
all I wished at the shooting star
is to somehow someone tell me that
she is the one.

"It's always him," she said,
"he is perfectly crazy as me."

She has phases like the moon
each with its own mystical
ways of brightness and
mystery was always dwelling in her eyes
the more I try to understand her ways
the more mystery arises.

There,
there I was looking at her—
contemplating
paralyzed without words
which might describe the beauty I see in her
the long hair flowing like a river
as the wind blows,
eyes as beautiful as of an angel
that holds all the universe inside it,
the skin that's like a smooth feather
lightest of all
bringing light to my eyes
delight to my soul and love in my veins

for the magic in her
I might die a thousand times
and born again
just to feel her once more.

Nothing else can make him happy
other than your smile
and nothing else can make him sad
other than your cry
because everything he does
is for you
only you
in celebration of you.

*I haven't came across more magical
thing that to love her and to witness at
the way she blossom in it.*

Mystery of her Magic

*LOVE ME LIKE THE WAY YOU LOVE
YOUR SLEEP.*

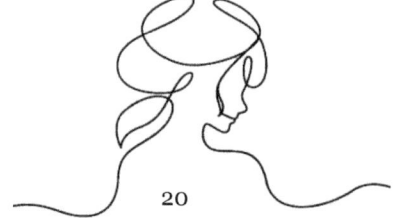

I wish I could scream and tell her about
how much I love her,
I wish I could sing and tell her about what
she means to me,
I wish I could just look into her eyes and
tell how beautiful she is,
I wish I could just make her stay a little
longer,
longer than forever,
I wish I could tell her that she makes me
a better person,
I wish
I just wish that she knows all these.

It is the desire that she provokes
to change myself
to be perfect for her
if it's wasn't for her
I will be imperfect forever.

She wore her smile like a crown and my kingdom bowed for her.

"SHE IS FOREVER BEAUTIFUL," HE SAID,
"LIKE CHOCOLATE DIPPED IN CHOCOLATE."

Let it break you bit by bit
piece by piece
like a tragic bliss
till someone comes along
and collect all those broken pieces
with their love.

It was the imperfection of my soul
and perfection of her soul that loved
we were just a means of
bringing them together.

She was just another soul that wanted to be loved and loved well.

They asked
"Why do you lover her so much even when you know it's going to end?"
"Because loving her is the only best thing I do." I replied.

It was the small things
about her I loved
like the way she tucks her hair back
when he comes in between her eyes.

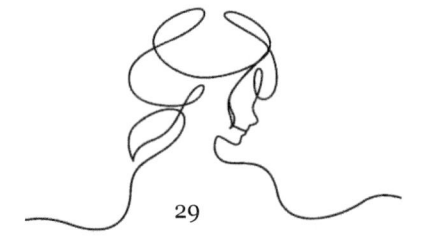

HER SHYNESS WAS HER BEAUTY.

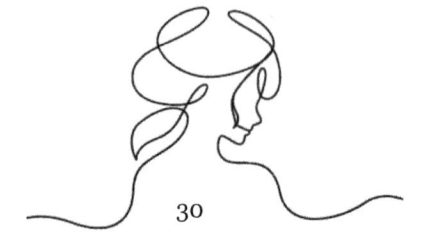

"I wish a little of you and a little of your love," He said
"No, actually.
I wish a lot of you and a lot of your love," He corrected.

Give her the freedom to fly
and then you will see an angel in her.

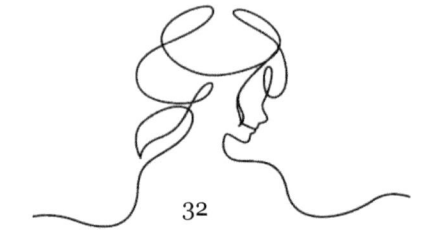

As she kissed me
I got a feeling of
being forgiven
for all of mine
previous sins.

Mystery of her Magic

You were like the star
bright,
beautiful and
light years afar.

I have spent my thousand days
thinking about all the thousand
little beautiful things you did

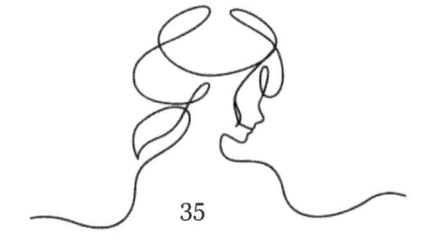

To the lonely man.
Don't you ever forget that you are
holding a flame in your hand
to bring the light needed into your life and
for those around you.

Her heart was so divine that my heart danced in heaven.

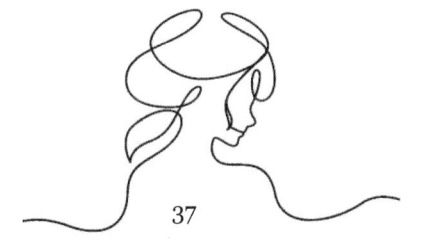

SHE WAS EVERYTHING HE SAID,
MY SILENCE BETWEEN THE SOUND.

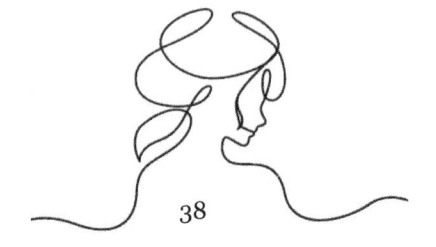

She is for me a warm place
with a little light
in a small town and a cabin
which is filled with all the things she loves—
Chocolate
tea,
cake
and momos.

Mystery of her Magic

To those who don't believe in magic
they just need to see the way
she tucks her hair back
they will start believing it too.

Every word I paint on the paper
is a way to make her
mortal soul
live immortal.

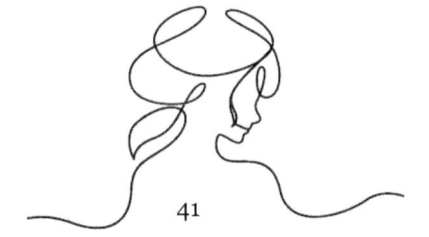

I will hold your hand my love
to the highest peaks of the mountain
and to the deepest depth of the ocean
I'll never let you go.

"She is like magic," He said,
"and with magic, there comes a lot of mysteries."

Mystery of her Magic

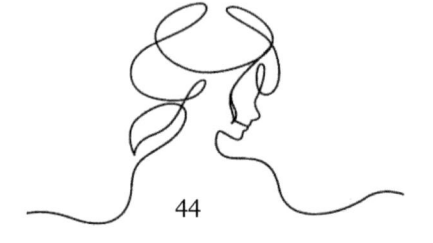

Sight of Love

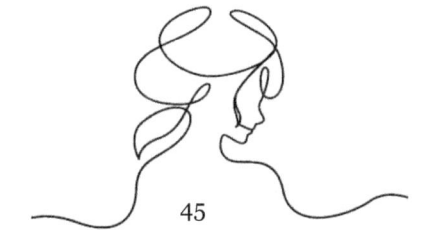

Maybe I will never find the escape
velocity of the gravitational pull of my
love for you, maybe I don't want to.

"I'm in love with a girl I can't have", he said
"we all are in love wit someone we can't have"
said the old man, "that's what get us up the next
morning, in the hope that someday we can."

Some people look good when they love
while some make love good when they love.

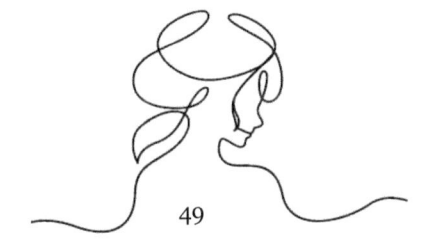

I held on to my broken heart
and hoped someone to find it beautiful.

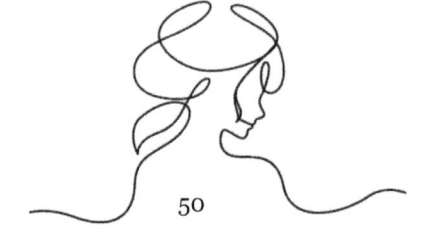

I'm in my dark abyss
as you put it
I don't need you to worry
I'll put myself back
until then hold me close
and tell me everything is going to fine
and I'll come alive.

I find more love with you
near a riverside
in a dimly lit town
sitting inside our cabin
with a perfumed candle
burning on the bedside
where you be reading a book
and I be telling you
of all the ways
I wanna seduce your heart.

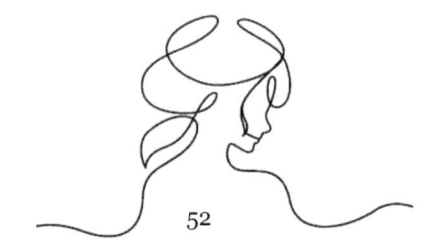

And from that day on he only slept after 1:43 am

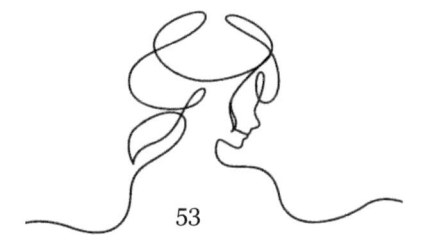

SOME GIRLS DESERVE THE LOVE OF ENTIRE UNIVERSE.

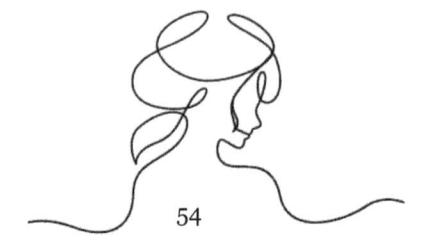

Of all the crossroads
I ever encountered
the one that leads to you
I have travelled the most.

I no longer need you
and that is the beginning of
I needing myself.

Venkatesh Ambati

She has her own darkness
taking toll inside her
but her light—
her light
was more brighter.

Mystery of her Magic

I am a slave of my love for her
seized willingly
just look at the light
I see in her
can't find a better reason to live life
other than for her.

In her laugh
I found the song that was
always running in my head
without a name
and when I heard her
it was like —
"Oh, there it is"

And she said
"your love is like sunshine in dark sky
but you my lover,
you are the nights knight like a vampire
you are sweet but dangerous
you are torn by your desires of
wanting to love me ever
and wanting to rip my heart out by
leaving me here."

one day I have you
next day your gone
but then someday we be
as if nothing is wrong.

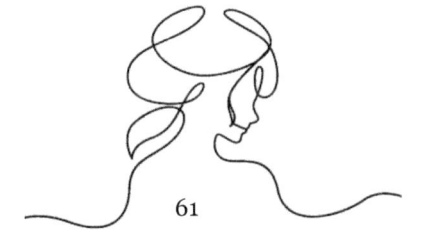

He was never to keep
like a storm and the rain
you have to let him pass
even if you love storms
but it's never safe to contain it
for all the damage it causes.

Three steps afar from wherever you are
I'll always be three steps afar
so that
if the thought of hurting you
crosses my mind
I have at least three steps
to change my mind.

Mystery of her Magic

Tell me what you love and I will forever
make your life swim around it.

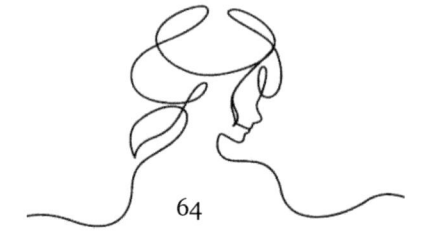

We wore love upon our coats
ready to get wet in the summer rain
singing and dancing along with peahens
hoping that it all will end with a
smiling rainbow.

Mystery of her Magic

You will never find a girl like her
in art, in poems or in songs
her magic was entirely different.

You are here with me in this eastern sky
it would a mistake if we don't dance.

It is always there, his love, always on her path waiting around the corner to make her feel loved at times when she needs the most.

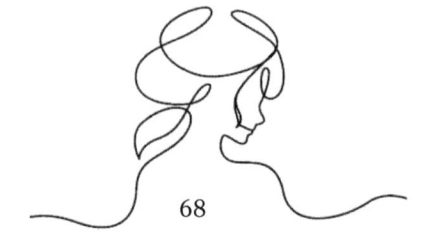

How cruel of him
while she was thirsty for love
he only shown her
the mirage of it.

Letting you go will be the death of me
so I held on and on
until I convinced myself
that I'm going to die
with or without you.

If love cannot save me from life,
well,
at least it will give me a peaceful death.

She feels something so close to heaven—
a serene place of love and happiness.

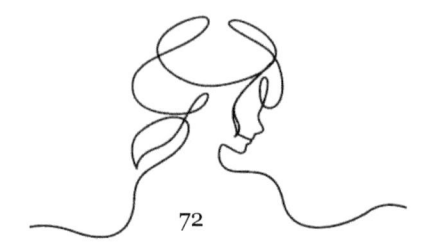

Love is toughest in the beginning
the wait the longing for other
to feel the same as you do.

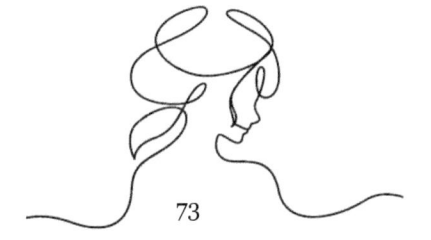

It's you in my life makes my life
worth a while
and dying doesn't scare me
because I have you,
I had you.

The way you kisses me
in between our talks
and in between the walks
like a surprise gift from a
beautiful friend.

In every rented breaths of my life I think about you.

I love her like night loves the moon—
fated for now and in phases forever.

I would race with you
to the end of our worlds
like two different shades of life
the dark and the light
where sometimes
as I lay down in my dark world
paralyzed in dirt
you stroke my hair kiss my head and say
"Everything's going to be fine."

And in the fresh perfume
of a burning candle
everything dark inside my soul
bewitched out of me.

It wouldn't be love if I let go,

by being told to let go or maybe it is.
hmm, who knows? I don't know, do
you? but I know this for certain that
there's something very pure about the
heart that holds on to the hope.

You are wrapped inside me so well that
only an exorcism can make me free.

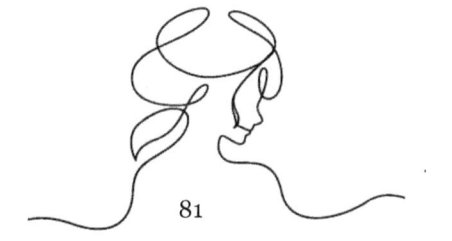

I would reincarnate a thousand times
after I die
on a promise that
I would get
one lifetime with you.

We sailed across our lives
from moment to moment
with dolphins and seahorses
kissing champagne on each other lips
fighting against the storms
that came our way
though we seemed crazy to the world
but our crazy was our love yacht all along.

She stayed all along by my side while I was a kind of mess flirting with my darkness.

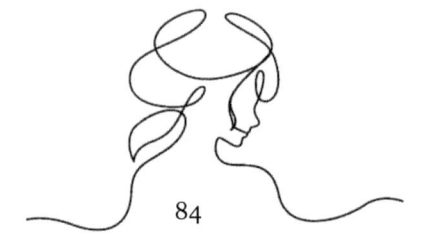

If you don't mend my heart I'll break yours too.

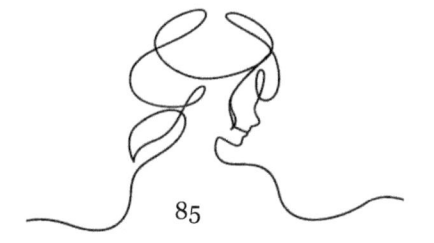

I am filled with a certain anguish that never goes and a immense desire to set fire to everything.

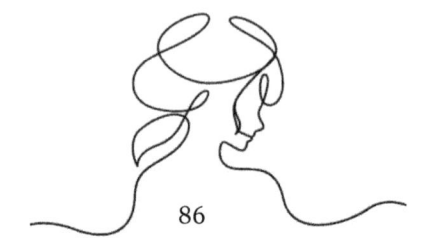

I always fancy girls like you He said, the
one who gets excited for sunsets.

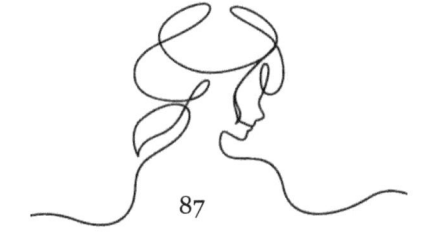

The only truth about me
you never knew is that
If it isn't you
I will wage war against fate for you.

And I always wonder
why I feel the things I feel
every time you are near me
as if I can't get enough of you
as if I was born just to be around you
as if I know you from an unknown dream
as if, if I'm not with you right now and for every next moments
I'll spend my time trying to
find the ways just to see you again
and again
and again.

And I always loved February and it's romantic dawn.

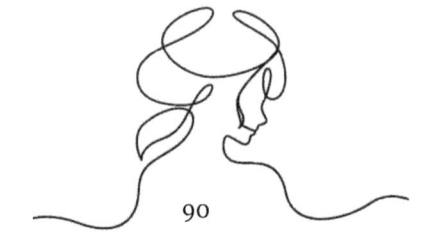

The closer you are to destruction
the better you feel
like a lone Rockstar
playing all the instruments
Although you know
it'll drive you crazy
but you can't help
but sit in that music.

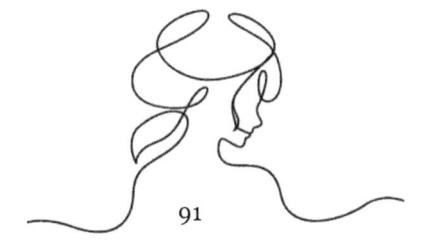

The biggest battle I ever had was to convince myself that she is not the one.

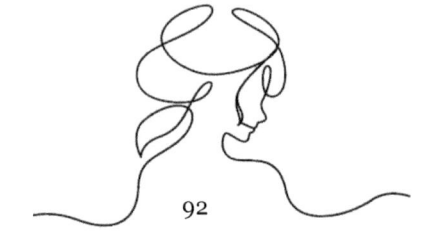

Ours wasn't the love like others
we were the muses of poets
like something out of the ordinary
something magical
something mystical
something beyond the world
a glance into a connection without a name.
We were lovers who hadn't made love,
yet,
but our souls has been constantly
Entwined
and tangled into each other's
and you know it.

Some truths are not meant to be said
and that is the truth.

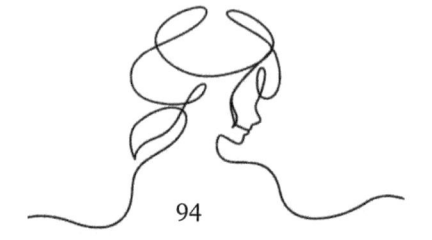

And I found in middle of the chaos,
there was you, an impeccable calm.

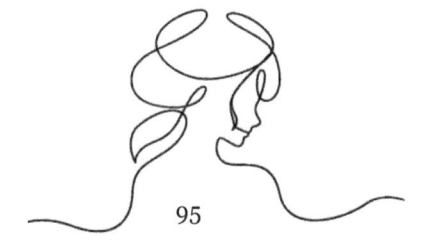

She wanted a world without me
and I owe her that,
but how can I ever make her know
that my world without her is nothing.

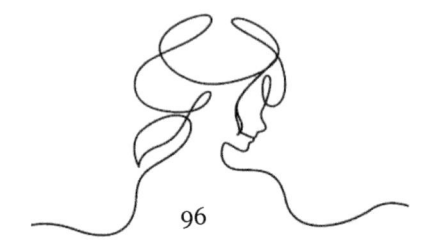

You, You are one of the perfect miracle
of this imperfect world.

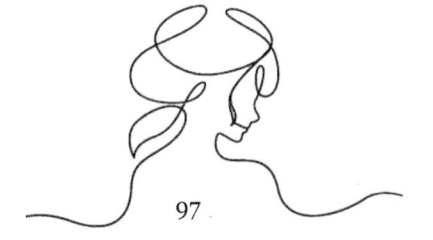

The road is black shimmering with tar
a carpet for the Angel of death
that walks upon it waiting for those
who slips into this tar pit trap
since he is
advertising a promise
of life without pain and
some self hating
manic depressive
and rebellious rockers like me
have always intentionally
or unintentionally
slipped their foot in it.

I was high on drugs and you were on life
It was an unknown truth at that time
even in such dizzy high

you were the only steady thing

I could see.

I'm constantly on the brink of
trying to forget you but every night is the same
where I do not sleep
and It's a lie to say that I'm moving on
because you're the only thing that I want.

It's hard to breath with a broken heart
I'm a angel falling apart
sweet darling let's not repeat our
love is a mistake if
it's more than a week.

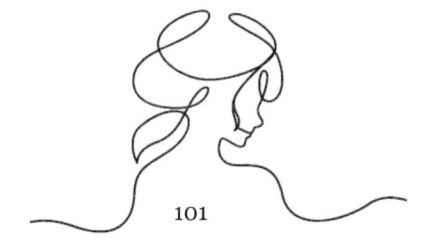

Sight of Magic

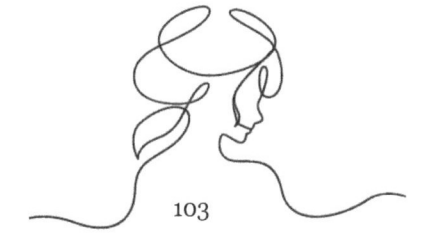

I was under the spell of your wavering
love ready to seize me for all eternity.

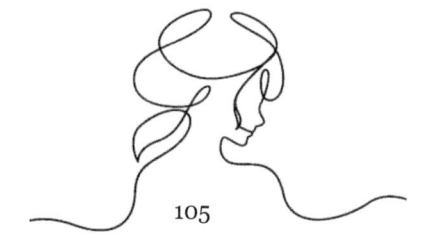

I try to understand myself every night
and I fail, I fail to the point where
failure gets upset on me,
so now I put myself
out of this misery
and conclude that -
I'm "EVERYTHING"
which is arguably
"NOTHING" after all.

In life
he said,
in every corner of the broken city
resides magic
in every song the morning bird sings
resides magic
in every cry of the newly born babies
resides magic
in every river flowing orphan hoping
to meet the sea
resides magic
in lovers arms
in friends laugh
and In families love
resides magic.
and even after all this magic
surrounding us
there's a whole damn ocean of magic
inside us.

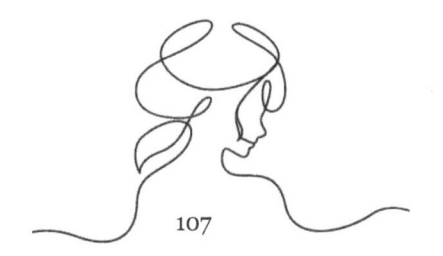

To all the voices in your head that say "you are not enough" tell them to bugger off because it's not they who decides It's you, always you.

Venkatesh Ambati

Take me down to the end of the road,
bring your knife with you, smile,
as you keep that sharp edge on my throat,
and tear me down from limbs to bones.

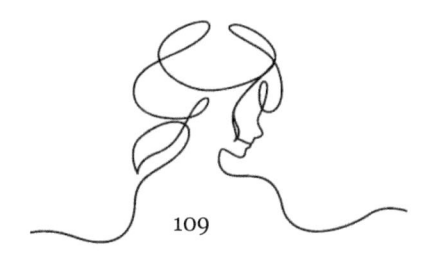

Sometimes it is like, you might die for her but she wouldn't care.

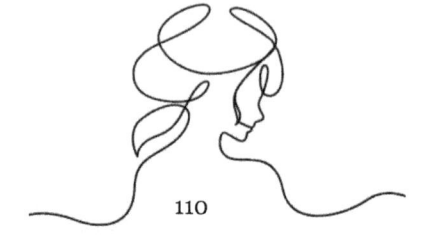

The hardest thing I ever had to do was to be myself.

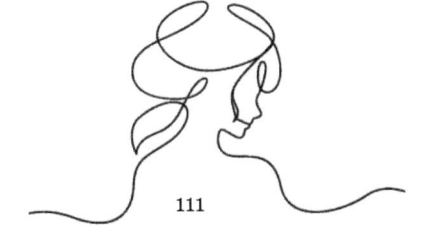

I'll trade all my days and sacrifice all my
nights to get one evening with you

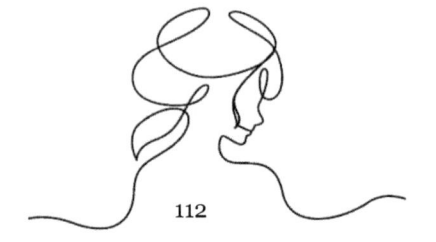

He asked,

Would you kiss me a thousand times
and tell me you love you if tomorrow is
the day I'll leave you?

Love could bring the worst in people and still be worth it.

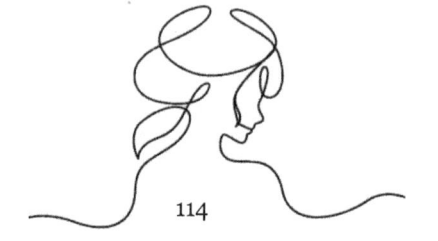

That's the thing about love - we don't want from those who love us, we want from those who don't love us.

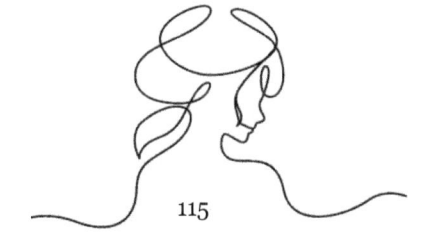

I wreaked your life apart with my
satanic fucking vibe
but you always loved me wholesome
in mirror of my disguise.

And you believed in me
that I could be a safe haven
since Satan was angel
before banished from heaven.

Live once or else you will die twice

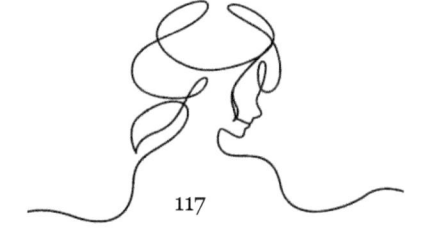

And when she left I felt a pang of a
something way more than loss.
It was like,
I couldn't hear the birds singing
I couldn't feel the warmth of the sun and
I couldn't see the stars shining,
thus fortune I knew it was the beginning
of my end.

There is no escape for me from the mystery of her magic.

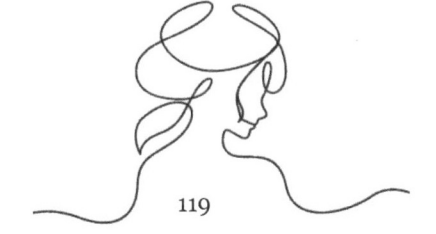

We tiptoed across the beach eating ice-creams and talking about the dreams of tomorrow.

A girl chasing her dream's is one of the unrecognized miracles of the world.

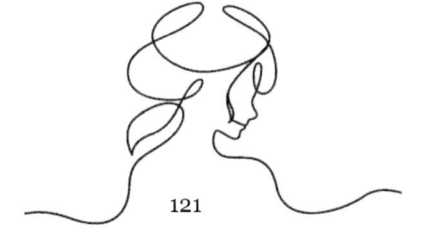

Mystery of her Magic

I know nothing of love but to kiss my girl
when she is mad feels very close to it.

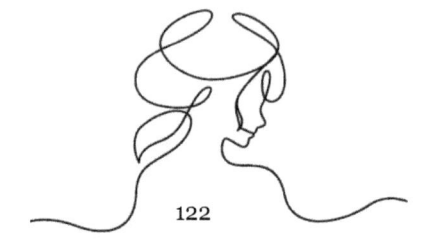

Venkatesh Ambati

She came to me
with colors I forgot existed clearing all the smoke
from every cigarette I burned telling me that
behind all the smoke
there is a whole beautiful soul I hide
And as quickly she came —
She wondered off to where she came from
telling me to remember her forever,
as if I could ever forget her

She didn't wanted anyone to save her
because she knows that,
her magic is way more powerful than
anybody's love for her.

She was a different kind of girl
not the usual who dances in the parties
kissing boys and whisky.
But the one when you look at her,
you stop for a while
and taking a deep breath you exhale -
"God, I could die for her right now."

Mystery of her Magic

We are caught in the mere adventure of our
romance of bright days and starry nights -
where in the dusk of this adventure we will
find our way back home,
together or apart,
who knows and who cares,
but for all our days we will live this
moment till eternity.

She wore the colour of moonlight more beautifully than the ivory white of Taj Mahal.

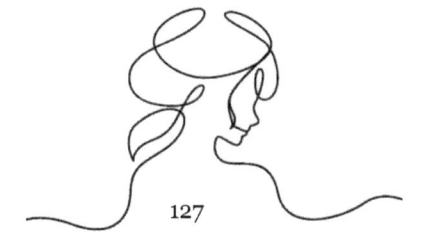

You were there always in front of me
    but a mile away and I was there
        hoping that you'd find me

Our love was a brief moment in time and space where everything was perfect.

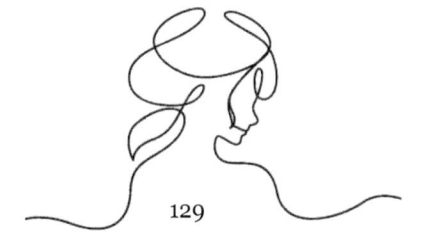

I will sail over the lake of fire
if I know at the end of it
it'll be You
I will get to see.

She was a perfect blend to all the imperfections in my soul.

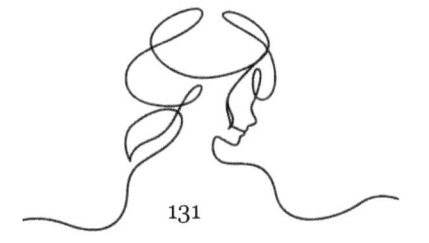

How foolish, being lost, when you don't know what you're looking for.

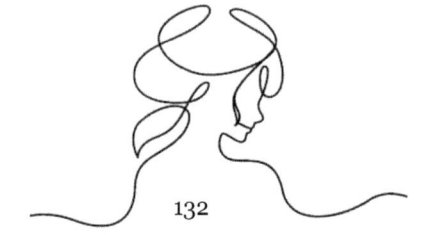

Love, for what it's worth can make a person go wild.

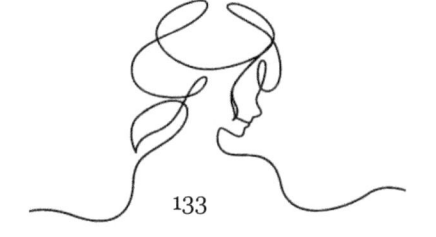

She walks around in love with the meadows not knowing that she is most beautiful of them all

And the darkness smiled, and said
"Here he comes again."

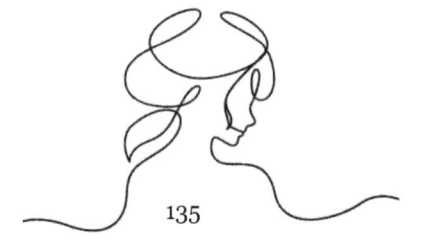

She could see demons in people
and yet she walks right past
as if she's the devil queen ruling them.

She will love you till the end.
If you let her be her.

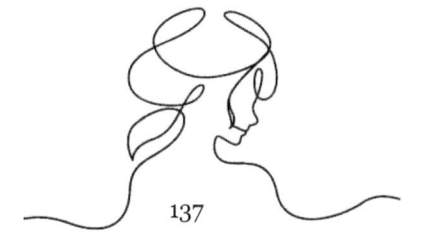

It wasn't just the chemistry of two
people liking each other but it was the
chemistry of two souls fused together so
perfectly that It would take an
apocalypse to separate them.

Once she starts talking she goes on for hours telling stories about every little thing, while I delight listening to her and find myself falling in love over and over again.

If you just look at the way her lips curl
while she talks, submerging herself into
each story re-

living it, will make you forget

every problem you have for a

moment.

She lives forever in these poems
and every time I miss her I re-read them
again and again
so that I can remind myself about
how she feels.

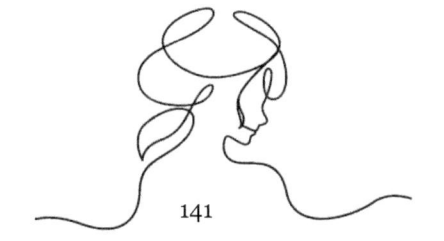

I'm forever yours! And forever is the least I could be.

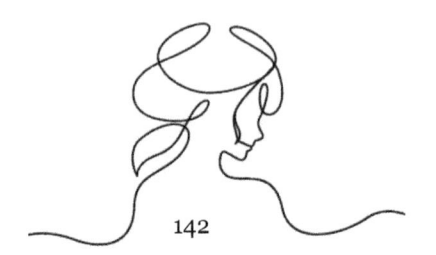

There is nothing more sparkling than a
girl who conquered her lonely nights.

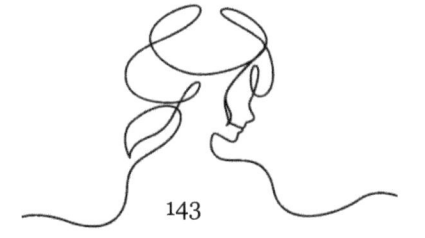

Mystery of her Magic

And I have to live knowing that you are the only one worth dying for.

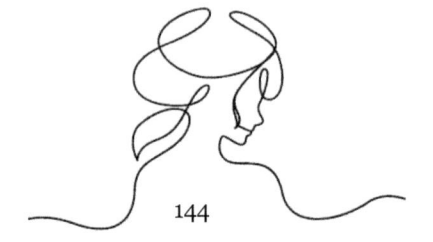

"What happens to the love when a lover die?" "It turns into the wind," said the man, "so that you can feel it all the time."

There is always a theory that love is like
a big bang in our heart forming stars,
galaxies and endless possibilities when
we find the one.

It was time to get ready

but she was facing the indecision

of choosing a dress for a day out.

Performing her own fashion show for herself

Can anyone advice her anything? No you can't,
she will not listen. And as time went by,

I think at one point

she took a look outside the window and
whispered to herself

"A sunny winter afternoon, ummm

a perfect weather to wear a sundress."

My dear, someday someone will love you the way you deserve - every second of the time.

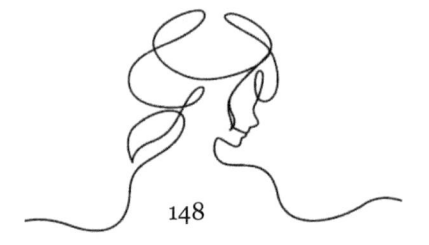

I want to be drunk on her smile rather than whisky and wine.

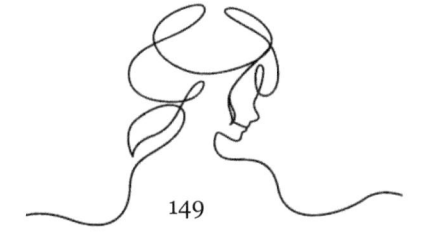

And every time they ask

"What is love?"
I find myself saying

"Mystery, just like her."

In every setting sun
as it sink inside me
I think about you for all the times
you calmed my storm.

She is kindest one I know,
sweetest one I adore,
everything right in this world,
everything perfect,
god's favourite angel sent from above,
that's why she is everything to me

There is every possibility that I am mad
but there is also the possibility that
I love you more than you could ever imagine.

Her eyes sparkle not as if they hold the stars
and the galaxies but an ethereal twinkle
enough to let you know she is magic.

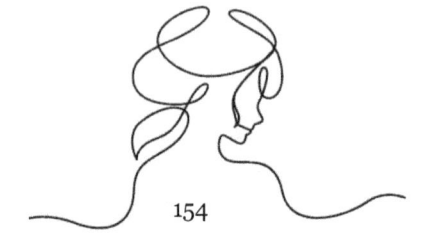

She is that lavender place
somewhere near
abandoned castles and empty fields
between the meadow of roses
and firefly light.

Milton Keynes UK
Ingram Content Group UK Ltd.
UKHW051410061024
449206UK00016B/114